For Maxine and Chris – J.C.

Copyright © 2012 by Good Books, Intercourse, PA 17534

International Standard Book Number: 978-1-56148-765-3

Text and illustrations copyright © Jane Chapman 2012

Original edition published in English by Little Tiger Press,
London, England, 2012

LTP/1400/0382/0412 • Printed in China

Library of Congress Cataloguing-in-Publication data is available.

I'm Not Sleepy!

Jane Chapman

Good Books

Intercourse, PA 17534, 800/762-7171, www.GoodBooks.com

At bedtime, Grandma always carried Mo up to the top of the tree.

"It's a long way up for a little owlet," she puffed.

Hop... Jump... Flutter...

Grandma smoothed the soft leaves
into a cozy nest and sat Mo
carefully in the middle.

"Play with me?" giggled Mo.

"No, Sweetie, it's time
for bed," smiled Grandma.
And she blew him a kiss
and hopped down to
her book.

The stars were fading when
Grandma heard a rustle.
"Is that you, Mo?"
"Yes! . . . I haven't had my
bedtime snack!"

"The bedtime snack! How could I forget?" thought Grandma, so she took one ...

Hop... Jump... Flutter... FLUMP!

to the top of the tree.

Grandma sat and waited
for Mo to finish his
bedtime snack.

"Play with me?" Mo snuffled,
between mouthfuls.
"No, Honeybun, time to go
to sleep," said Grandma.
And she blew him a kiss and
hopped down to her book.

The last bats were going home when
leaves began to rain down from above.
"Mo," Grandma called, "is everything
all right?"

"No! ... And I'm not tucked in!"

"He's not tucked in!" sighed Grandma. "Up we go."

FLUMP!

Hop ... Jump ... Flutter ... FLUMP!

...right to the top of the tree.

Grandma plumped and prodded...

and tucked and rolled ...

until Mo looked like a
wriggly green pancake.

"Play with me?" he laughed.

"No, Pickle, it's BEDTIME," said Grandma.

"No more noise now ... unless there's an emergency." And she blew him a kiss and hopped down to her book.

Grandma sat in the stillness.
All was quiet at last. She was
just about to start reading when ...

"GRANDMA, GRANDMA!
IT'S AN EMERGENCY!"

"IT'S AN EMERGENCY!" thought Grandma. "Oh my goodness!"

"What is it? What's the emergency?" puffed Grandma.

"I'm not sleepy!" said Mo.
"I don't want to go to bed.
I want to play!"

Grandma squeezed into Mo's cozy nest next to him.

"The thing is, Mo, it's bedtime, and at bedtime SOMEONE has to go to bed," she said. "So, I have a very good idea. I'LL go to bed, and YOU can stay up!"

"YES! YES! YES!" laughed Mo, "and you'll need fresh leaves ... and a bedtime snack ... and tucking in ... and EVERY TIME I come up, I'll blow you a kiss."

Mo was very busy.
He didn't have time to play.
It was hard work putting
Grandma to bed.

Hop... Jump... Flutter... FLUMP!

Hop... Jump...

Flutter…**FLUMP!**

FLUMP!

Flutter…**FLUMP!**

Hop…Jump…**Flutter**

Most of the stars were gone when a little voice called up from below. "Grandma?...I'm really sleepy." "Of course you are, Poppet, it's very late!" said Grandma.

And she hopped down the tree to her favorite owlet. "On my back," she said.

Hop...
Grandma carried Mo...

Jump...
all the way up...

Flutter...
to his nest...

FLUMP!
at the top of the tree.

Grandma snuggled Mo down
and folded soft leaves over him.
"Time for bed," she smiled.
Then Grandma smoothed Mo's
feathers gently, blew him a kiss,
and hopped back down
the tree to her book.